Waiting For Claudia

And Other Mazes

by
Tim Grotrian
and
Justin Grotrian

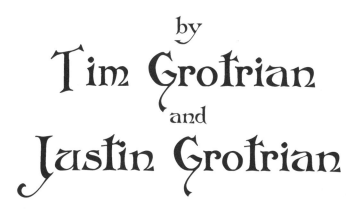

Cover Design: David Grotrian
Inside Design: Sam Finocchio
Cover Color: David Grotrian

Visit Labyrinth Productions online at
www.labyrinthproductions.net

Order this book online at www.trafford.com
or email orders@trafford.com

Most Trafford titles are also available at major online book retailers.

Printed in the United States of America.

ISBN: 978-1-4669-8435-6 (sc)
ISBN: 978-1-4669-8472-1 (hc)
ISBN: 978-1-4669-8436-3 (e)

Library of Congress Control Number: 2013904170

Trafford rev. 03/19/2013

   www.trafford.com

North America & international
toll-free: 1 888 232 4444 (USA & Canada)
phone: 250 383 6864 ♦ fax: 812 355 4082

Foreword

"In einem entlegenen Schloss ausserhalb der Stadt Klausenburgh wurde eine merkwuerdige Entdeckung gemacht." Burgermeister von Klausenburgh 18~~. ("In a remote castle outside the city of Klausenburgh a strange discovery was made.")

With these words by the Mayor of Klausenburgh, Romania in the 19th century, our story begins. It is a strange account that will leave more questions unanswered than answered, so if the reader likes stories that are tied up in neat tidy packages, then this is not the manuscript for them. The research done for this book continues at www.labyrinthproductions.net. There, the reader will not only find a continuation of the narrative, but also rules for solving the puzzles presented in this book. So enjoy the journey. Life, after all, is a mystery. Is it not?

For My Sister Lisa

The other two books in the Labyrinth series, Light Your Way and The Lost Book, are available for purchase at

www.labyrinthproductions.net

Table Of Contents

Part I

Part II

Maze Solutions

Part I

Strange Discovery

"In einem entlegenen Schloss ausserhalb der Stadt Klausenburgh wuerde eine merkwuerdige Entdeckung gemacht." Burgermeister von Klausenburgh, 24 June, 18—

In a remote castle outside the city of Klausenburgh, a strange discovery was made. There, a book was found that gives an account so fantastic, I hesitated to make it public for fear I would be doing more harm than good. Also found was a painting of a Count who lived in this region many years ago, and who some feel is still alive today. This painting shows the Count in his library. I believe this book came from this library.

I will begin with a drawing of the castle. The vault, the heavy door of which was unlocked so as to make entrance possible, shows where the book was located.

It is important that this work be come to light, for if the events presented within are true, and I believe they are, then these beings may still be alive and must be found, confronted and revealed!

Mayor of Klausenburgh, 24 June 18——

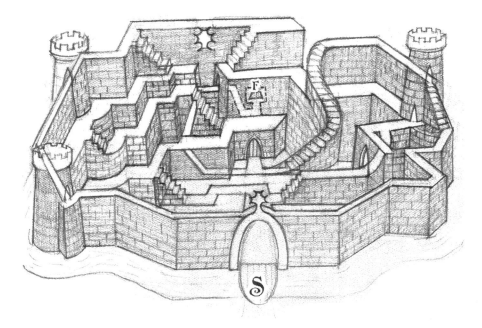

The Birth of the Daughter

Account Written by the Attending Physician,
Klausenburgh, Romania   February 20

On the 20th of February I presided over the birth of
Claudia D., daughter of the Count. I was awaken from my sleep
by an emissary to the Count who gave me instructions to fetch
my medical bag and come with him. The emissary presented such
a terrible image that I simply froze in my bed, gaping at him. As I
hesitated, he suddenly presented a dagger. He pressed this dagger
to my neck, the pressure of which led me to my utensils and then
to the carriage that was to take me to the Count's castle. The
countryside of Romania has been so ravaged by war that I saw
many unbelievable sights along the way, and I will tell you the
tale of the "Forest of the Impaled" is no tale, but rather the truth,
because the roads were lined with bodies run through with long
stakes and then set out on display for any would be invaders to
contemplate.

As we approached the castle, I heard the dreadful howling
of wolves and the barking of what must have been huge dogs, for
I could not even hear the galloping of the horses due to their echoes
off the Carpathian mountains.

The passes were so narrow, I thought at certain times we
would go headlong over the cliffs into the abyss.

When we finally arrived, the horrible sounds had stopped and I stood at the entrance of a truly magnificent palace. The castle's stone steps and hallways were illuminated by torches making it easy to find my way. Once in the Count's presence, I quickly bowed and removed my hat. I had heard the stories told by the townspeople of visitors who had forgotten to remove their hats, and how He, offended by their rudeness, had then nailed their hats to their heads!

In a rather spacious room that was dimly lit by the torches, I found a young woman whose countenance both fascinated and frightened me. She was remarkably pale with the blackest hair and the lightest grey eyes. Her appearance was so strange that I had to fight the impulse to react in a negative way. I was lucky that I did not, for the Count was in the room, barely visible in the torchlight. His eyes were dark, and he didn't say a word, but rather motioned for me to get on with the delivery of the child.

The mother showed little emotion. Even though slight of build, she was remarkably strong, and at one point, she grabbed my arm during the act of giving birth. I later noticed an abrasion where she had held my arm in her vice-like grip. All this from a woman whose body weight could not have been more than 110 pounds!

I was amazed at the quickness of the birth. In less than 45 minutes, a girl was brought into the world. I examined the child as well as I could, for the light was dim.

She seemed quite healthy, but there was one thing that bothered me greatly. The child was born with teeth!

The Reflection

From The Diary Of The Count, June 24

My little Claudia is growing up wonderfully. She is so smart. Her tutors are amazed at her abilities in the arts and mathematics. I have purposely kept her from any hint of astrology or the supernatural. I have even tried to give her a good grounding in the natural sciences. Science. Now there is an interesting subject. I don't think there is anything in any science treatise that would explain the phenomenon that is us. She knows that we are different, but she doesn't quite know how. One of her tutors is worried about her obsession with her reflection. It seems she goes to the lake in the meadow and stares at her reflection for long periods of time. I myself am not worried about her looking at her reflection excessively in the lake, but rather if that reflection would disappear. We all know what that would mean.

Night Walks

It is a disturbing trend that I see. That trend is my little Claudia being more and more in love with the night. She is tending towards getting up late and neglecting her lessons. The "Lighting of the Candle" has become a nightly routine. And then comes her wanderings through the forest. And where she wanders. I have warned my charges to keep their distance. I watch her on her walks, as far as that is possible, but she gets away from me at times. It is as if she knows I am there and does everything she can to elude me, for her nature is rebellious. I am worried.

Narcissistic?

Diary Of The Count, September 13

It has come to the attention of those of us in the castle that Claudia spends much time gazing at her reflection in a mirror that was locked away in one of the castle's abandoned towers. She even carries it with her into the forest, so she can look at herself in the moonlight. The word being spoken around here is that she is "narcissistic". Coming from our kind, that is so funny. After all, if some of could enjoy our reflections, I'm sure we would. So, I can understand her obsession with the mirror. After all, without the mirror we really don't have any idea of ourselves. We reflect nothing. Think about it.

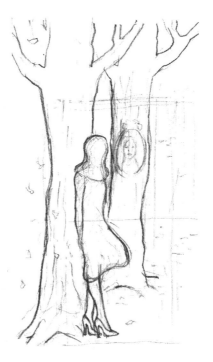

She Is So Beautiful

From the Diary of the Count, March 4,

She is so beautiful....my one and only. I love her so and cannot bear the fate to which she is doomed. I have tried everything, but I cannot reverse the curse which is ours. I'm hoping somehow that it will skip her, that she will be spared. If she does start to manifest the symptoms, I do have a plan that will allow her to escape. It will be painful to implement, but she must survive!

Marie Auf Der Heide

The writings of a peasant father.

I will never understand how such a fate could befall one so innocent. She always loved her walks in the countryside, picking flowers and listening to the songs of the birds. And she was always so curious. No matter how dangerous it was, I simply couldn't keep her away from that castle with all of its legends and tales. I told the girl numerous times not to wander off and above all, not to go near that god forsaken place. "That Count is mad!", I told her, but did she listen? Well, you see the results. My wife and I have grieved, and it is so horrible not to know her fate. Oh, she came home alright at one point, but she had changed, so pale, so utterly distant. Trying to keep a watch on her was useless. It would always happen at night, you see. We resolved to keep her in her room, in her bed, so she could sleep. There came a time, however, where we had no control... that look, that stare! We were paralyzed! We even enlisted the help of the local pastor, but after dealing with our daughter for an evening, he told us that whatever was possessing her was beyond him and that exorcism was not his expertise.

She eventually never returned from her midnight wanderings. I thought at first that his guard dogs or those howling wolves had gotten her. But I then heard that she was seen near the abandoned tower in the Carpathian mountains. I tried to see if it was true, but even though I know the forest like the back of my hand, I couldn't find it. It was like a spell had been cast over the tower which made it disappear!

I Could See It In Her Eyes

From the Diary of the Count, October 31

What else could I do? I had to take the life of a peasant to save my own blood. She was such a common girl. She will never be missed. Someone should have been watching her anyway. Who could know?

I could see it in her eyes that it was meant to be. She didn't even resist when I took her in. It was like she wanted it. Now the townspeople are all alarmed because she is missing. They had ample opportunity to protect their little Marie Auf Der Heide, but didn't. Now I need her. Things are closing in, and I need this peasant girl to help me see my plan through. I am afraid they are finding out that there are moments when we are vulnerable. Under all circumstances, my little Claudia must survive and Marie will help me make it so!

It's Too Late

It's too late. The curse is upon her. I so hoped she would be spared, but there is nothing I can do. The plan I have must work. It will be difficult to let her go, but I must. The fortress outside of Klausenburgh will be her haven until such time has come. I will move her in the dead of night so as to not arouse suspicions. The South Tower will be perfect for her. These townspeople, as stupid as they are, do have ways of outsmarting one. They will not outsmart me! I will not let them. She must survive! She must!!

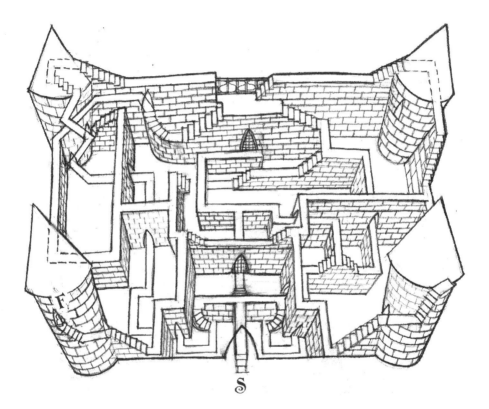

Is She Dead?

From an article published in the Klausenburgher Zeitung (newspaper) by the journalist Herr Karkov

Klausenburger Zeitung

Grave Watch

Claudia, the daughter of the feared Count, has been laid to rest on castle grounds after a long illness. Even though her father was the most powerful person in the region, no one came to the burial of this young girl. It must be said that there was something strange about this girl and the entire situation surrounding her death. Indeed, it is the underlying sentiment that she is not dead, but that somehow she will come back. Therefore, a young man armed with a large crucifix has been assigned to go to the cemetery and keep watch over the grave. Is this just superstition or is there something to fear?

Franz Karkov

Resurrection

Account given by Serto N. concerning the gravewatch.

I did my very best. I was awake the whole time, even though it is being reported otherwise. I was nodding off, I admit, but I heard the heavy stone being pushed aside and I awoke. It was then I saw her! I couldn't believe my eyes. It was our own Marie pushing away the stone covering the grave. I called out to her, but then she looked at me with a stare so mesmerizing, I couldn't move. It was like watching everything through a veil. She then gathered the body of the Count's daughter from the grave, placed it on the ground, and as she looked at me again, the young Claudia just rose to her feet as if she hadn't died at all! This girl who just a few hours before had been laid to rest, was up and walking! Why, she walked right past me while our little Marie watched! It was a Resurrection!!

The Vault of Claudia

The Vault of Claudia is in the fortress I prepared for just this occasion. I have kept this secret dutifully, for I believe the townspeople have arranged search parties to find her since the "Resurrection". Ha! Resurrection! Such superstitious people! They have no idea what they are dealing with. And even if they do, there will be little they can do to stop it. With their little Marie guarding her coffin, let them try! They don't realize that she is capable of tearing them limb from limb! And they think I am violent! It was just dumb luck that I was able to lure her in so easily. And now she is watching my little Claudia until I can send her to her new home! And Marie will be her escort!

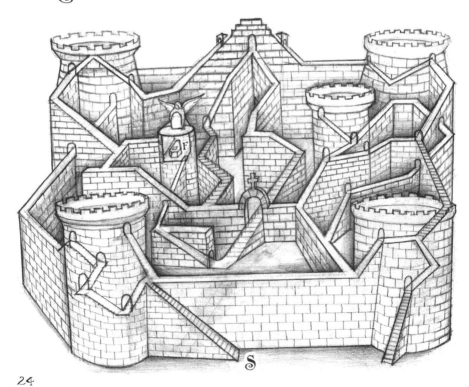

24

The Prison Of No Return

Journal of a Bavarian Mercenary, 14 March

We captured her, the little Marie Auf Der Heide. Little?! It took ten of us to subdue her and three of them didn't survive the fight with "little Marie"! In fact, they were ripped almost beyond recognition! What kind of a being is this? You won't believe what then happened. After holding her for only a day, the guard simply opened the gate for her! He says she called to him and then he doesn't remember anything after that. And not only that. The others simply let her find her way out. They said it had something to do with her eyes, her stare. And now she is on the loose again. This shows me that the "Hexenjagd" (witch hunt) was justified. How else can you explain this?

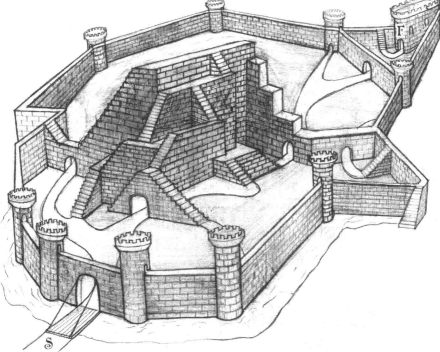

The Mirror

Letter From Sylvia L.To Veronika L.

I realize you have to flee. The authorities are after all the wrong people. Of course, I feel bad for all those innocents, but the chance of detection is too great, and it is better to let the situation be what it is, rather than revealing ourselves by resisting them.

The "Chateau Dubrovnik" is ready and waiting for you. This time you need to take up residence there and wait out the purge that is sweeping our land. I am old and will not be able to follow you to your new home. I will do what I can here to help some of these girls survive, but after you move, I want you to stay in Dubrovnik and sharpen your powers. If what is happening here is any indication, the purge may spread, and your being on the other side of the Adriatic will ensure your survival. Therefore, I am willing you the most potent weapon in our arsenal, "The Mirror", whose powers you already know.

The chateau is complicated, but you will eventually find "The Mirror" in the back on a stair landing. I keep in out in the open, rather than under lock and key, because the more a secret is allowed to be a part of the natural fabric of the environment, the less suspicious it is. This is an axiom that you will understand in time and which will become important to you later. For now, though, keep the mirror right where it is and don't let anyone stand in front of it too long, otherwise, it will be impossible to stop the transformation that is taking place.

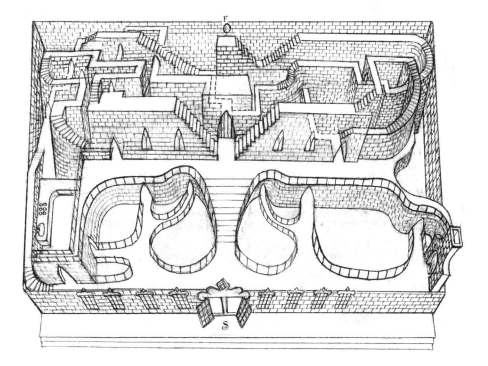

Coastal Chateau

Diary of the Count, February 4

In my despair, I am making a journey to a particular girl who it is rumored to have survived the awful "Hexenjagd" (Witch Hunt) that is sweeping through the provinces of Germany and taking the lives of so many innocent, young girls. If the stories of supernatural powers and magic are true, and it is my deepest wish that they are, then through them I spy a kind of hope. A hope that my little Claudia will be saved. Therefore, I will travel by night to the coastal city of Dubrovnik on the Adriatic where this young witch is said to have a Coastal Chateau. I will see if it is in her powers to help with my dilemma. I don't need to tell you that I fear no man, but to tell you the truth, I go to this house with great trepidation, because if the stories that I hear concerning this girl are true, then her powers are great and one has reason to fear. But then, that is why I am going to her!

In The Family

I felt sorry for all of those girls. They had nothing to do with anything. The men going after them are so weak, so threatened. And the outrageous accusations; spells, sorcery and what not. What do they know about it? It was hideous they way they tried to get them to confess. All of those methods of torture! What kind of mind comes up with those things! They didn't even know what they were to confess to. At the end, the girls were saying anything just to avoid the "Third Wheel". It kills them you know, that "Third Wheel"! And now they are talking about the "Scheiterhaufen". (Burning at the stake.) These authorities have no idea what they are doing. There is no telltale sign, and those of us who do know these things, have ways to avoid detection. When they came to my door, I simply looked them in the eye and used the words that work every time. It runs in the family you know. Our powers are passed down, and a few threatened men are

not going to stop us, torture or not. Besides I have the mirror. I left Germany and came here so as not to provoke them and cause more deaths among those innocent girls. But why is he coming? His reputation is one of the worst in all of Europe. If he thinks he can harm me, he is mistaken. I and my family will handle him too, just like all the others.

The Agreement

Letter from Veronika L. to Aunt Sylvia, June 24

The meeting began sinister enough. He insisted for reasons that I understand now, that it take place at night. He also asked permission before he entered our Chateau. There seemed to be something important in this, and, because I detected fear, I went along with this ritual and formally granted permission for him to enter. Can you imagine. Him afraid of me!

His request was not unreasonable. I told him I could ensure safe passage, and we agreed on a fee and protection of our kind in the provinces he controls. He asked me how I could ensure safe passage, but I told him that would be a secret I could not divulge. He tested me on this point, trying to stare me down, and then his assistant, the powerful little peasant girl, also tried, but to no avail. They don't understand the origins of our magic, and within a few minutes they could see it was useless. I think he wanted to see the extent of our power, and needless to say, I convinced both him and the little one. Now it is underway, and thanks to the family secret, I can certainly take his precious daughter to her new home. It won't be pleasant for the others who are involved, but I am extracting a huge benefit from him, so what must be done, must be done. It is a matter of business and that is all.

Part II

Setting Sail

Captain's Log From the ship "Dubrovnik", July 10

We set sail this morning from the port of Dubrovnik and, with a good wind at our backs, will spend a day in the Adriatic before we reach the Mediterranean. From there, it will all depend upon the weather as to how long it will take to reach the Atlantic. We have plenty of rations, for it is a long journey to the Port of Boston.

My crew is good. They do what I say, because they know I will not tolerate any slacking or mischief. We work 24 hours and have to rest in an intelligent manner, so as not to become so tired that we lose our bearings. The mind has to be considered on a journey as long as this, since it can play tricks on one, if one is not careful. And since we work "24", it is up to me to see that this doesn't happen. We are off to a good start, and I have my Bible and my rabbit's foot with me to see that it stays that way!

Strange Cargo

Captain's Log, July 21

I've been spending time in my cabin researching the records concerning our cargo and those who ordered its shipment. Normally, I don't inquire into the people who commission my vessel, but I must say, the circumstances surrounding our cargo are so strange that I feel I must. I have found only a certain Marie Auf Der Heide on the schedule with a Count D. listed as the sponsor. About Ms. Auf Der Heide, there is nothing, but the latter does have a reputation, and I'm thinking that since the cargo is not ordinary freight, but rather locked in a single room, it must be either gold or precious stones. Whatever it is, I cannot but think it is extremely valuable, for the girl gave specific instructions that it was to remain locked the entire journey, and that we would be met by a person to be named at the time of our arrival in America to release it.

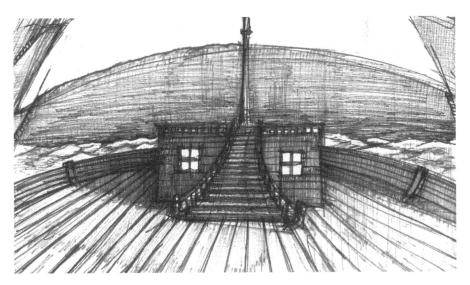

Hallucinations

It is becoming clear to me that our America mission is being complicated by several crew members who are having hallucinations that there is some person or thing on board stalking them. They will no longer go below deck, not even to the galley, because of this fear. They stay above deck with wild looks in their eyes staring out to sea, mumbling that they have to get off the ship before the "Thing" gets them. I've seen the tricks that long journeys play on the minds of sailors, but this is something different. It must be a type of brain fever that is causing them to go mad! Even the sea itself is rising up, as if in anticipation of some type of impending doom!

Dance of Death

The strangest site confronted me as I was awakened by the commotion of accordion, percussion and stomping feet. I hastily dressed myself and rushed to the deck to find my crew members writhing in the moonlight to the beat of the percussion and accordion. It was the type of dance that I have seen in the tribes of Africa before sacrificing one of their own to placate evil spirits that they feel are surrounding them. It turned into a "Dance of Death" because it culminated with some of the sailors actually throwing themselves overboard into the black sea below! And now I cannot get the crew to go below deck. They keep talking about "the presence" that is lurking there and asking, "Who will be next". What they mean by this, I do not know, but I attribute it to the brain fever that I suspected when these hallucinations started.

Surrounded By Insanity

Captain's Log, August 17

I have lost control of the situation. I am surrounded by insanity. The crew, or what is left of them, no longer responds to my orders. They lurch about, wild eyed, looking around as if this "thing" is lurking around every corner. Threatening them with the plank or hanging seems as if it would be a relief compared to being confronted by 'the thing'. The problem is, I have felt its presence myself!

I am unable to eat or sleep. I am surprised I am even able to write in this journal. The journal! This document will become very important should we not survive this journey. And it is appearing more and more likely that that will be the case!

It Is Finished

This is my last entry. May the person or persons who find this journal be able to shed some light on what has happened here. I am going to lash myself to the wheel in a desperate attempt to get us to land. God help us.

"The Thing" is walking openly among us now. It is finished. The ship is hers.

Plague Ship

From A Pirate's Journal, September 3

It appeared out of nowhere through the fog. The lookout saw it as it just drifted with no visible sign of life.

We got the ropes and lanterns and went out to her not knowing what we would find.

We worked our way up the ropes and onto the deck. I thought it may be some type of trap. The merchants do that, you know. They hide under deck and then surprise us as we climb up the ropes.

Well, we climbed on "at the ready", with swords and pistols drawn.

I would be lying if I said it didn't chill me to the bone (Or should I say, "Shiver me timbers".) when we fanned out on deck expecting a fight, but instead just stood there with nothing but the sound of the waves. No one! Not a single soul seemed to be on that ship!

Carefully, we made our way to the wheel, and it was clear that someone had lashed himself to it, for the lashings were tied to the captain's coat. The coat though, was covered with blood and ripped apart, as if the captain had, well, been ripped apart right there! What form of man or beast could have done such a thing? Or did the captain do it himself?

We then found the stairs that led to the deck below.

It was dark as we silently made our way through the labyrinth of passageways that finally took us to a long corridor, where evidently, the crew slept. I led the way, but when I got to this corridor, I just couldn't go any farther. It was inexplicable. It was as if I was paralyzed. I wasn't, of course, but there was some force which kept me from going on.

Could it have been something supernatural that cleared the ship of its crew? I really didn't want to remain any longer to find out. Anyway, there was nothing in the way of monetary value that would compel us to stay. By the way, the ship was not entirely devoid of life. There were rats. And well, after the "Black Death", we've had enough of rats. So, I gave the order to leave.

Waiting For Claudia

Letter from Veronika L To Count D., Sept 4

I saw them enter and I saw them leave. There was no way they were going to get near your little Claudia. The "Strange Cargo" as the Captain called it, was something they never could have imagined. And now she, along with her helper little Marie, is on her way to a whole new world. And that world is waiting...

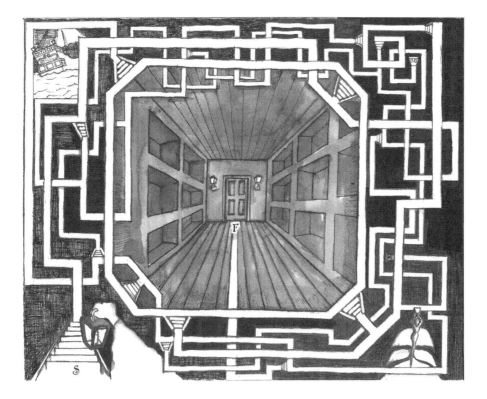

waiting...

waiting for Claudia.

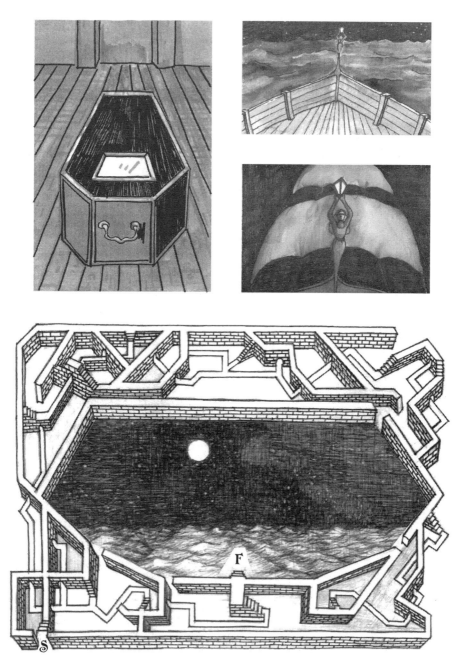

The End

Maze Solutions

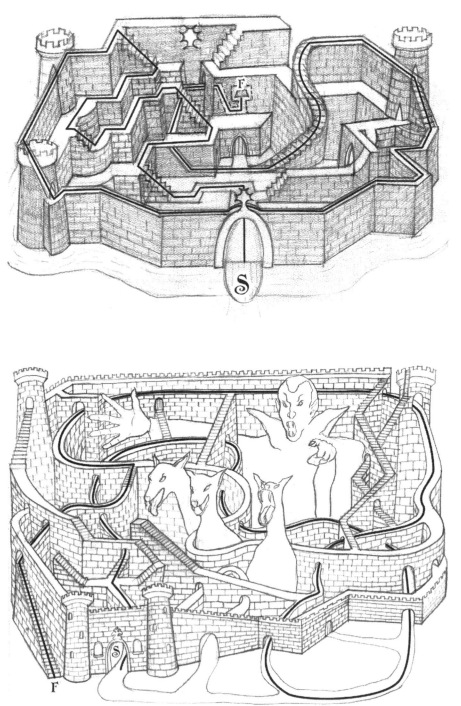

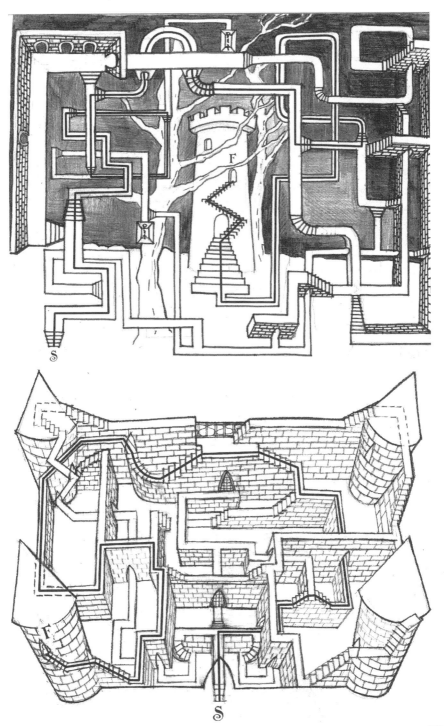

49

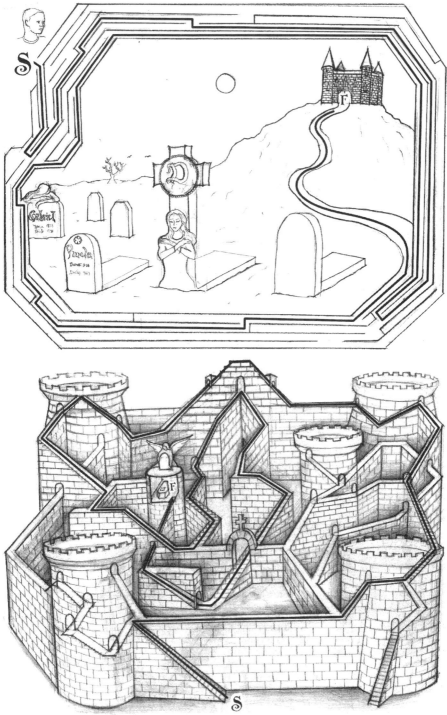

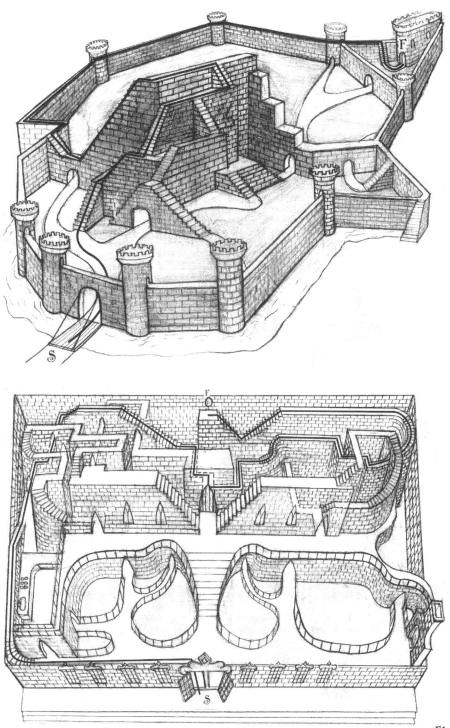